Welcome to...

THE MAMMOTH
ACADEMY

NEAL LAYTON

Henry Holt and Company · NEW YORK

Henry Holt and Company, LLC
Publishers since 1866
175 Fifth Avenue
New York, New York 10010
www.HenryHoltKids.com

Henry Holt® is a registered trademark of Henry Holt and Company, LLC.
Text and illustrations copyright © 2006 by Neal Layton
First published in the United States in 2008 by Henry Holt and Company
Originally published in Great Britain in 2006 by Hodder Children's Books,
a division of Hachette Children's Books
Library of Congress Cataloging-in-Publication Data
Layton, Neal.
Mammoth Academy / Neal Layton.—1st American ed.
p. cm.
Summary: Woolly mammoth siblings Oscar and Arabella enjoy being at
Mammoth Academy, but Oscar is accused of stealing oranges and when he follows
some mysterious tracks to find the real thief, he discovers humans living nearby.
ISBN-13: 978-0-8050-8708-6 / ISBN-10: 0-8050-8708-7
[1. Woolly mammoth—Fiction. 2. Mammoths—Fiction. 3. Schools—Fiction.
4. Brothers and sisters—Fiction. 5. Prehistoric animals—Fiction.
6. Prehistoric peoples—Fiction. 7. Glacial epoch—Fiction.] I. Title.
PZ7.L4476Mam 2008 [Fic]—dc22   2007046935

First American Edition—2008 / Designed by JRS Design
Printed in the United States of America on acid-free paper. ∞

1 3 5 7 9 10 8 6 4 2

For Anne McNeil
—N. L.

OSCAR

ARABELLA

SOME OF THE OTHER
PUPILS AT
THE
MAMMOTH
ACADAEMY

← FLY LIVED IN
THE ACADEMY BUT
WASNT A ~~FOOL~~ PUPIL.

CAVE
CAT

ORMSBY

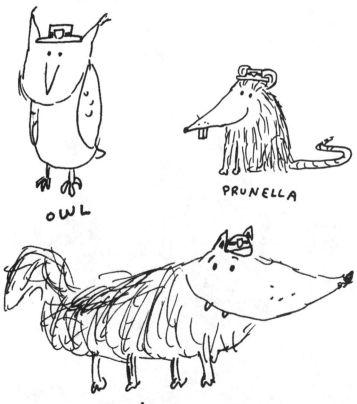

OWL

PRUNELLA

FOX

A FEW MORE PUPILS OF
THE MAMMOTH ACADEMY

RHONDA

REGINALD

REMI

ROGER

REX

RUFUS

REENIE

GIANT
GROUND
SLOTH

CAVE
BEAR

CONTENTS

1.
WELCOME TO THE ACADEMY

Oscar was a woolly mammoth, and so was Arabella. They lived a long time ago in the Ice Age.

They used to spend their time making ice sculptures, exploring caves, and doing all the other things that young mammoths like to do. But there comes a point in a young mammoth's life when it's time to grow up a little bit and start school.

Oscar wasn't looking forward to it. He didn't want to be cooped up in a classroom and told what to do.

Arabella, on the other hand, was really excited. She loved the idea of learning new things and making new friends.

One day, a Very Important Letter arrived—by mammoth mail, of course.

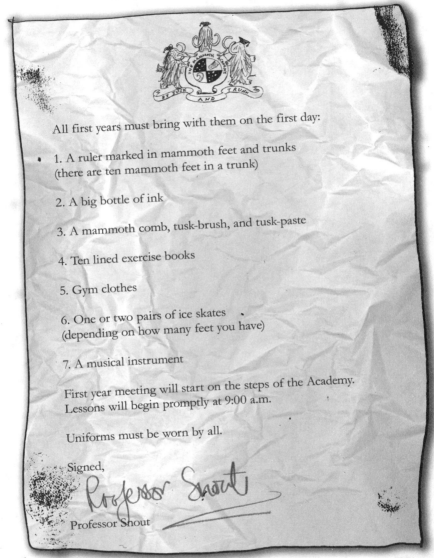

All first years must bring with them on the first day:

1. A ruler marked in mammoth feet and trunks
(there are ten mammoth feet in a trunk)

2. A big bottle of ink

3. A mammoth comb, tusk-brush, and tusk-paste

4. Ten lined exercise books

5. Gym clothes

6. One or two pairs of ice skates
(depending on how many feet you have)

7. A musical instrument

First year meeting will start on the steps of the Academy.
Lessons will begin promptly at 9:00 a.m.

Uniforms must be worn by all.

Signed,

Professor Shout

Professor Shout

↑ THIS IS OSCAR'S COPY OF THE LETTER. ARABELLA PUT HERS NEATLY AWAY SOMEWHERE. OSCAR SHOVED HIS UNDER HIS HAT.

That first morning was cold and crisp—and very snowy—as the animals left their homes to walk across the icy wastes to the Academy.

There was a friendly Megaloceros to help them across the glacier and signs to make sure they didn't stray over the cliff into the marsh.

It seemed to take a long time to reach the Academy, especially with Oscar dragging his big feet, but eventually they arrived at the gates.

In the yard was a noisy throng of animals of all shapes and sizes. Oscar and Arabella recognized a few faces, but most of them they had never seen before.

Suddenly a gong rang. BONG! BONG! BONG! BONG!

On the steps stood the head-mistress. She was quite a stern-looking mammoth, not at all like the old auntie mammoths back at the herd. But when she smiled her eyes twinkled.

"Welcome," she said. "Here are your maps and schedules. Off you go!"

And that was it. Oscar and Arabella's new school life had begun.

The West Wing

Professor Bristle's Classroom

Concert Hall

More Classrooms

HERE IS ARABELLA'S COPY OF THE MAP. AS YOU CAN

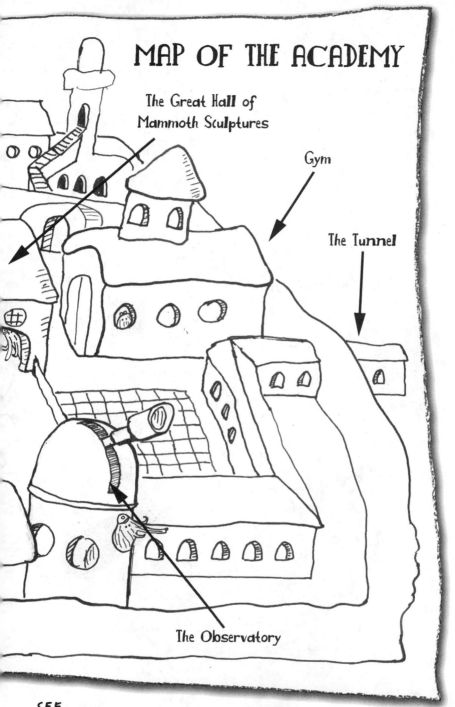

MAP OF THE ACADEMY

The Great Hall of
Mammoth Sculptures

Gym

The Tunnel

The Observatory

SEE SHE HAS KEPT IT NEAT AND TIDY.

t Wing

Professor Bristle's
Classroom

Hall

More Classrooms

↑ THIS IS OSCAR'S COPY OF THE MAP.

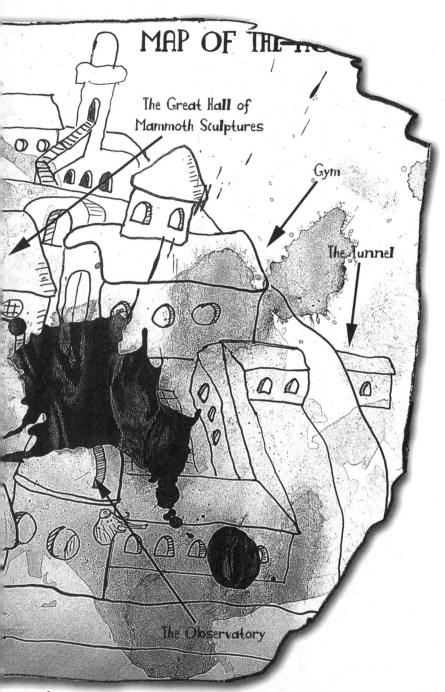

MAP OF THE H

The Great Hall of
Mammoth Sculptures

Gym

The Tunnel

The Observatory

(I THINK HIS BOTTLE OF INK
MIGHT HAVE LEAKED IN HIS BAG)

2.
FIRST LESSONS

Oscar's first lesson at the Academy did not go terribly well. To begin with he was late. Somewhere in the West Wing he had a disagreement with Arabella over the best way of finding Professor Bristle's classroom.

Oscar had insisted that he knew exactly where he was going. Arabella had insisted that his map was upside down and he'd better follow her if he had any hope of arriving on time.

Having decided to strike out on his own, Oscar found lots of interesting things to look at . . .

. . . before finally coming across the MYSTERIOUS TRACKS.

Now, if you saw MYSTERIOUS TRACKS, what would you do? Oscar decided to follow them (of course!).

They were quite faint due to the heavy snow-
fall and disappeared altogether in places, but here
and there were little bits of orange peel that were
easier to spot.

Eventually the trail led him to a big warm room
that smelled of baked cakes and cabbage.

"Hey, you! What are you doing here?" shouted
a scary-looking mammoth. She was dusted with
flour and waved a rolling pin in her trunk. "I hope
you're not the young scamp who's been stealing
oranges from the pantry."

"Errrrr . . . um," mumbled Oscar.

The big mammoth plonked the rolling pin down
and picked Oscar up by the scruff of his neck.
"Right. You're coming with me!"

And so Oscar arrived at Professor Bristle's
class—late, covered in flour, and with Cook ac-
cusing him of stealing oranges. All the time he
was trying to explain about the MYSTERIOUS
TRACKS and the orange peel . . . but not getting
anywhere.

Professor Bristle didn't seem too interested
in what Oscar had to say either. He merely told

Oscar to dust himself off, take a seat, and apply himself to the mathematical problem written on the blackboard.

The only seat left in the class was next to a fox that Oscar didn't know. Across the room, Arabella was sitting next to Ormsby, the woolly rhino. He was having a good chuckle about Oscar's scruffy state. The rabbits seemed to think it was quite funny, too.

"Don't worry," said Fox. "I'll help you catch up—and what's all this about MYSTERIOUS TRACKS? It sounds terribly exciting!"

Oscar immediately felt like he had found a friend.

3.
MORE LESSONS AND JOKES

After that, Oscar's first day seemed to go a little more smoothly. They had exciting lessons: Geography, which was interesting.

THE ICE SHEETS

THE MAMMOTH LANDS

MORE ICE

THE WORLD

A GLACIER

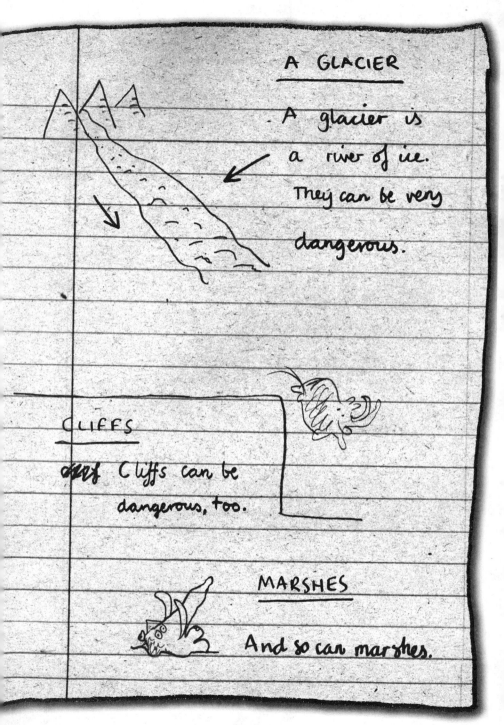

A glacier is a river of ice. They can be very dangerous.

CLIFFS

Cliffs can be dangerous, too.

MARSHES

And so can marshes.

Skiing, which Arabella enjoyed.

And music.

Oscar and Fox particularly enjoyed the music lesson.

Until eventually—BONG! BONG! BONG!—it was time to go home.

On the way home Oscar introduced Arabella to Fox, and Arabella introduced Oscar to Prunella.

As they walked, Prunella talked about all the problems of being a small mammal in the Ice Age and which of the rodents she thought was cutest at school. Arabella thought Prunella was great.

And Fox told them lots of jokes that Oscar found hilarious.

"What's the difference between a woolly mammoth and an orange? You can't comb an orange!

"What's the difference between a woolly mammoth and a currant bun? A currant bun doesn't weigh two tons!

"Can a woolly mammoth jump higher than a mountain? Yes, mountains can't jump!

"Good-bye! See you all tomorrow!"

4.

OSCAR'S THEORY AND FOX'S GREAT IDEA

The next morning at the Academy there was a special assembly called for all the staff and students.

It seemed that during the summer holiday, when the Academy was closed, somebody had broken into Cook's kitchen and stolen nearly the entire year's supply of oranges.

This was very upsetting news indeed, since mammoths were very fond of oranges.

The headmistress made it clear that anyone who knew anything about the orange theft should tell a teacher immediately.

After that, things became a little difficult for Oscar. Teachers would sit him in the front of the

class and give him the "I've got my eye on you, so don't try anything" look.

And if Arabella, Prunella, or Fox introduced him to any of their friends it would be as "Oscar, the one who Cook thinks stole the oranges," because news at school travels fast.

Oscar thought he'd better try to solve the mystery.

That evening on the way home Oscar was quiet and thoughtful. Professor Bristle's lesson on addition had him thinking.

$$1 + 1 = 2$$

The strange thing about the MYSTERIOUS TRACKS was that the animal appeared to have only two feet, and therefore two legs.

Oscar knew of only a few animals that had two legs.

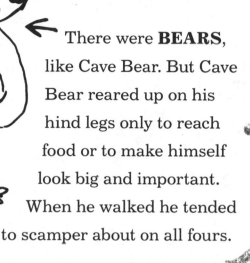

There were **BEARS**, like Cave Bear. But Cave Bear reared up on his hind legs only to reach food or to make himself look big and important. When he walked he tended to scamper about on all fours.

And there were **OWLS**. Owl could walk on two feet, but he didn't do it often because it was much easier to fly everywhere. And, in any case, his feet didn't make tracks like the ones Oscar had seen.

This left only . . .

...HUMANS!

But everybody knew humans were more likely to eat animals than oranges, and, as Arabella said, nobody would take the idea seriously unless Oscar could provide some PROOF.

Oscar wasn't about to give up on the idea yet, though. The next day at playtime he suggested that they all play a new game called Catch the Orange Thief by Finding More Tracks.

At first it was tremendously popular, but when no more tracks were found, the others grew bored with the game, so Oscar decided to drop it.

With no more thefts reported, interest at the Academy moved on to other matters. Like inventing stand-up-wheeled-sleds.

Oscar, Arabella, and all their friends enjoyed outdoor sports, especially sledding. But if a traditional sled hit a rock or a bit of mud where there wasn't much snow, it would stop. This is where Oscar's invention came in.

STAGE 1

FIRST OF ALL HE GOT AN OLD BIT OF WOOD AND STOOD ON IT.

STAGE 2
WHEELS ARE ADDED...

THE INVENTION MK II

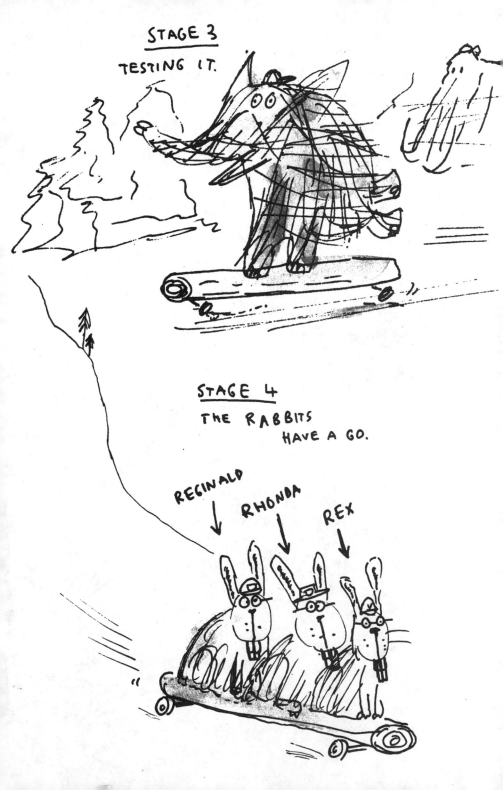

Not everyone was convinced, especially after the rabbits crashed headfirst into a tree, but Fox remained a firm supporter. In fact, due to his enthusiasm for just about everything, Fox had quickly become Oscar's new best friend at the Academy.

Fox was also full of interesting ideas.

Every afternoon after gym with Mr. Strong, Mrs. Mop would make sure all the animals had a good hot shower, followed by fur (or feather) drying and fur (or feather) brushing.

Fox was less than keen about the whole thing. What was the point in having to wash every day at the Academy, and then dry yourself, and then having to brush your fur after you'd dried it, and then having to do the same thing all over again when you got home?

"But you don't wash much at home," said Owl.

"No," admitted Fox. "But, listen. I met this

warthog the other day who said that after about two months of not washing you don't need to wash at all. Your fur just naturally starts to clean itself. And all of a sudden you don't smell and you don't have to wash ever again. Doesn't that sound great?"

The others had their doubts about Fox's great idea.

"Well anyway," Fox continued, "starting from today I'm not going to clean myself at all, and then in two months or so I'll be self-cleaning, and life will be great!"

Fox seemed quite pleased with himself.

Oscar wasn't convinced, though. He didn't like to say it but Fox didn't smell that nice at the best of times.

The first thing that happened to Fox on his first "stop washing ever again" day was that the caretaker accidentally emptied kitchen slops all over him, but this didn't put Fox off the idea. Far from it.

"Now that I've stopped washing, it doesn't bother me at all. In two months I'll be as fresh as a daisy."

5.
HUMAN STUDIES

Oscar was beginning to really enjoy life at the Academy. He had a particular talent for sports, and Mr. Strong was very pleased with Oscar's efforts

on the ice lake. Arabella was also good at ice skating, and the two of them enjoyed skating fantastic routines together, much to the amusement of the rabbits and Ormsby.

But the lesson that everyone enjoyed the most was HUMAN STUDIES.

"Of all the animals, the one to be feared the most is THE HUMAN," said Professor Snout. "This is what a human looks like. Ugly-looking brute, isn't he? And this is the female of the species.

"Their cubs are called children, but don't let

their size deceive you. They're probably the most dangerous and tricky of them all."

The class shuddered.

Where they live:

In caves and primitive huts.

They leave tracks like these...

...and droppings like this.

And they eat <u>YOU,</u>

all of <u>YOU,</u>

except your wool and bones because after they have eaten you they'll wear your wool and make a ~~hat~~ house out of your bones.

WOOLLY HAT

HOME SWEET HOME

Oscar was thoroughly intrigued by the lesson, making little notes in the margins of his notebook and imagining what it would be like to come face-to-face with a real human, when his attention was drawn to something outside the classroom. It looked like the trees had been jostled.

Oscar put down his pen and peered out the window. All of a sudden about fifteen or twenty faces appeared at the icy glass and then quickly disappeared. Faces EXACTLY like the ones Professor Snout had been drawing on the blackboard!

"Sir. SIRRR!" shouted Oscar with his trunk
and three feet in the air. "I've seen humans, sir.
I've seen a whole bunch of them!"

"Yes, I know, Oscar. I've been drawing them on the blackboard for the last half an hour."

"No, I mean I've just seen REAL HUMANS! RIGHT OUTSIDE!"

6.
TRUNK TROUBLES

Professor Snout did not sound the special alarm gong or call all the students to arms. All he said was "Well, that's impossible, Oscar. There aren't any humans for miles around here. I've heard the rumors you've been spreading about the MYSTERIOUS TRACKS and the orange thief and all the rest of it, but it simply isn't possible.

You probably just saw a wild boar rooting in the bushes.

"As I was saying, humans are the most dangerous animals in all mammothdom."

This was a little too much for Oscar. At lunch break he sneaked out of the playground with the rest of his classmates to look at the area outside the window.

There didn't seem to be any signs of human activity though.

asked Prunella.

said Fox.

said Arabella.

chuckled Ormsby.

It was snowing wet slushy snow, but that didn't stop Oscar. He kept looking throughout the rest of lunchtime and evening playtime, too.

And all the way home, and all around the herd until after dark.

He continued looking the next morning, all the way to the Academy.

By the time he got to class it was as plain as the trunk on his face that Oscar was not well.

For starters he kept sneezing.

"Hi, guys! How are . . . ATCHOOOOOO!"

And then there was the trunk-blowing.

And the weepy eyes.

And the woolly hearing.

Poor Oscar, everyone thought. He must have been coming down with a cold, imagined he'd seen something out the window in his half ill state,

SNIFF
SNIFF!

and then good and properly gotten sick with the
sniffles after all this silly searching.

Even Oscar admitted that he may have been overdoing things.

Arabella suggested they get him some nice soft leaves to blow his trunk on. Professor Snout gave her permission to go off to collect some. It took several hours but at last she came back with a big heap, and it seemed to help.

Owl and Cave Cat thought it might be a good idea to put Oscar's feet in a bucket of hot water and so, with Professor Snout's permission, they went off to collect some snow, which they took to the kitchen for Cook to heat. That seemed to help, too.

Ormsby thought some blankets might be a good idea, so he spent a couple of hours collecting wool from around the place, which he knitted into a lovely warm blanket. This seemed to help, too.

Professor Snout went out to forage for some berries to use to make some hot berry juice.

And then Oscar ran out of soft leaves to blow his trunk on, so Fox and Arabella went out to collect some more.

Gradually over the week, Oscar felt much better.

SNIFF
SNIFF

The same could not be said of his classmates and teacher though.

Sniff.

Sniff.

"Atchooooo!"

Later that afternoon in the nurse's office . . .

7.
THE MOUNTAIN TRAIL

With the cold and muddy weather and the shortage of oranges, it didn't take long for the whole Academy to come down with the sniffles. Even Cook was sniffling and sneezing but somehow managed to keep going, making gentle little meals of scrambled eggs and prunes for everyone.

Oscar was feeling much better though, and he had got to thinking about the humans again. Perhaps he had been mistaken after all. Perhaps the faces he saw at the window had been because he was sick.

It had been really kind of his classmates to look after him when he was feeling poorly. It was the least Oscar could do to find some berries and soft leaves to help get everyone well again. He took his stand-up-wheeled-sled invention to carry the berries and leaves back.

Oscar hiked into the forest to collect leaves. Then he held them under his arm as he sledded down the slope to put them in a pile at the bottom. It was very exciting.

He climbed farther up the mountain, following a little track. The descent was even more thrilling now. He could take the jump at the bottom a little bit faster and fly a little bit farther.

"Wheeeeeeeeee!"

Oscar decided to climb even higher up the mountain.

Then, a couple of minutes' walk up the track, he came across some footprints. They were similar to the ones he had seen on his first day, except these looked fresher. There was a clearly defined outline of a foot, which looked identical to the diagrams in Professor Snout's class. It was a HUMAN FOOTPRINT!

PROOF! The proof he had been looking for!

Humans here, in the valley!

This left Oscar with a difficult choice: he could either rush back to the Academy now and tell everyone, or he could follow the tracks to see where they led. What did Oscar decide? I bet you can guess!

The footprints continued up the mountainside, and at times they got quite muddy. Oscar had also begun to notice pieces of orange peel or some banana skin or cherry pits. This human had been snacking all the way and leaving the litter to prove it.

Oscar began to feel a little nervous. He was about to turn back when, suddenly, he was hit by

the most terrible smell! It was like dung smeared
with rotten cabbage and stinky cheese. It was so
pungent it made his trunk smart and his eyes
water, but it was also vaguely familiar.

"FOX! What on earth are you doing here?"

"Well," said Fox, "I decided to visit everyone in the nurse's office, but nobody seemed pleased to see me. They insisted that I go and find you. Cave Bear even gave me half his sandwich if I went, which I thought was most generous of him. Would you like a bite?"

Oscar decided not.

Fox was so stinky now that most of the animals at the Academy tried to avoid him. Even Oscar tended to stand upwind of him if possible. But he was glad to have a friend along with him.

Slowly they trudged onward and upward, following the muddy trail of footprints and orange peel and discarded pits higher up the mountain,

until eventually another set of footprints joined the original set of tracks.

So now there were two Humans.

A little farther up, another set of tracks joined the first two.

Soon more tracks appeared from the undergrowth, until it was impossible to say how many there were.

"Perhaps we ought to hop on my invention now and warn the others," said Oscar.

"We could," said Fox, "but we've come this far, so we might as well carry on a tiny little bit farther, even if we are scared."

About twenty yards up the hill the forest opened into a clearing where the tracks led right up to a cave.

The friends decided they would tiptoe across the clearing, take a quick peek in the cave, and then immediately turn tail and launch themselves down the mountain on the sled. Even if they were spotted they would be able to get back to the Academy much faster than any human could run.

So Oscar and Fox nervously tiptoed up to the cave entrance and carefully peered around the corner.

8.
CAVE SKOOL

In the cave some young humans were having lessons. They seemed to be very excited.

Oscar and Fox crept a little farther inside the cave to get a better look. This is what they saw.

On the walls were some badly spelled bits of writing along with primitive stick-like drawings.

LESSON 1

WE NEEDS TO EAT FOODS OR WE ~~HO~~ GET HUNGRY.

FOODS WE EAT

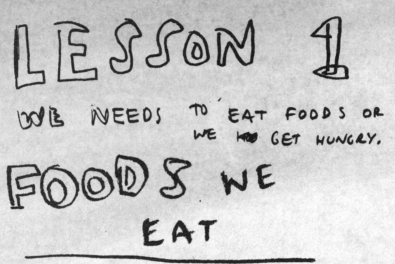

THE <u>INSIDE</u> OF ROUND ORANGE THINGS

(THE OUTSIDE TASTES HORIBLE)

THE <u>INSIDE</u> OF LONG YELLOW THINGS

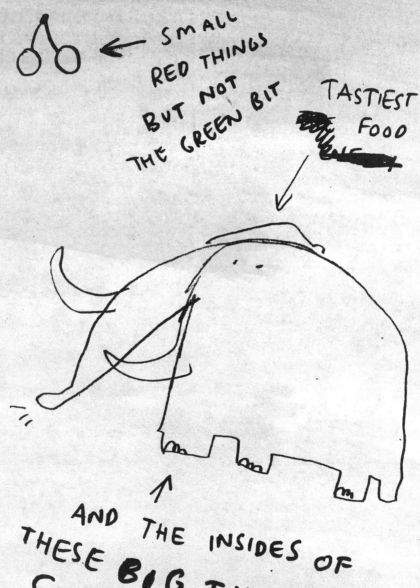

LESSON 2

~~HOW TO~~ CLUBS

AND HOW TO MACE THEM.

THIS IS A CLUB →

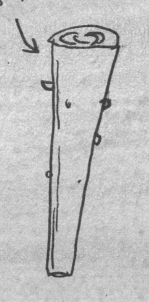

YOU
MAKE A
CLUB BY
GETTING A TREE,
BREAKING A
BIT OFF.

CRACK!!

DON'T MAKE
YOUR CLUB
TOO BIG

OR
TOO
SMALL

THINGS THAT
CLUBS CAN
BE USED FOR

① SMASHING
   THINGS
② HITTING THINGS
③ SCARING
   THINGS

So the humans had stolen the oranges from the Academy!

Around the cave were clubs of all different shapes and sizes. It didn't take Oscar and Fox long to realize the danger.

Not only had a tribe of humans set up a cave school in the mammoth lands, and not only were they stealing fruit from the kitchen, but they were planning a hunting trip to get some FRESH MEAT! The Academy must be warned AT ONCE!

Oscar and Fox began to back out of the cave. But Fox wasn't feeling well. He was feeling a little bit sneezy.

"Ahhhh . . . ahhhhhhh . . . ATCHOOOOOO!"

Standing in the cave entrance was a huge, enormous human waving his fists and growling. He seemed very upset.

UGHHHHHH!

The human picked up the wheeled-sled invention and—CRASH!—bashed it down into the ground, splintering it in two. He advanced toward them, still clutching half the sled in his fist.

9.
TRAPPED!

By now the rest of the cave school had spotted them, too.

"Ugh. Ugh. UGH!"

Professor Ugh started grunting orders at his pupils, who formed a ring around Oscar and Fox and forced them back into the cave.

"Are they going to bash us with clubs and eat us?" whispered Fox, nervously.

"No, I think it's worse than that," replied Oscar. "I think they're going to keep us here while the rest of them attack the Academy and eat our friends and teachers, and then they're going to come back here and bash us with clubs and eat us for dessert."

"Crumbs," said Fox.

Oscar and Fox looked on helplessly while the rest of the humans went to pick up their clubs and organize themselves into a hunting pack.

Everything seemed to be going according to plan, except for one human who was having a problem picking up his club. This was probably because it was at least seven and a half times the size of him. Eventually he picked up a twig and went to join the others.

The hunting party began marching off down the mountain toward the Academy.

Meanwhile one enormous human was left to guard Oscar and Fox.

The friends sat down in despair, desperately looking for a way out.

In the middle of the cave was a huge roaring fire. Oscar thought that the humans must need it

to keep warm, since they seemed to have very thin coats, but it was making him and Fox a little hot and sweaty.

In fact, because they were upset and worried, they were sweating much more than normal. And Fox was beginning to get very stinky indeed. It was becoming a bit too much for Oscar to bear. He pinched his trunk shut and tried to think of nice things like flowers and the smell behind Arabella's ears.

The huge, enormous human guarding them seemed to be having an even harder time. He was holding his nose and trying to hold his breath. Every now and then he had to gulp down some of the toxic air, which made his eyes bulge and caused him to clutch his throat and shudder.

And then Oscar had an idea.

This proved too much for their guard, who yowled like a scalded cat and fainted with an almighty THUDDD!

Now was their chance. Oscar and Fox ran out of the cave, but the hunting trip was long gone. Even if they ran their fastest they would never get to the Academy in time to warn the others.

There was only one thing to do.

It was no wonder the stupid human had been unable to lift the giant club. Together Oscar and Fox could barely heave it even a few inches off the ground, but eventually they managed to attach the four wheels from Oscar's invention to the bottom.

It took a while to get it moving, but once it got going it seemed to pick up speed surprisingly quickly.

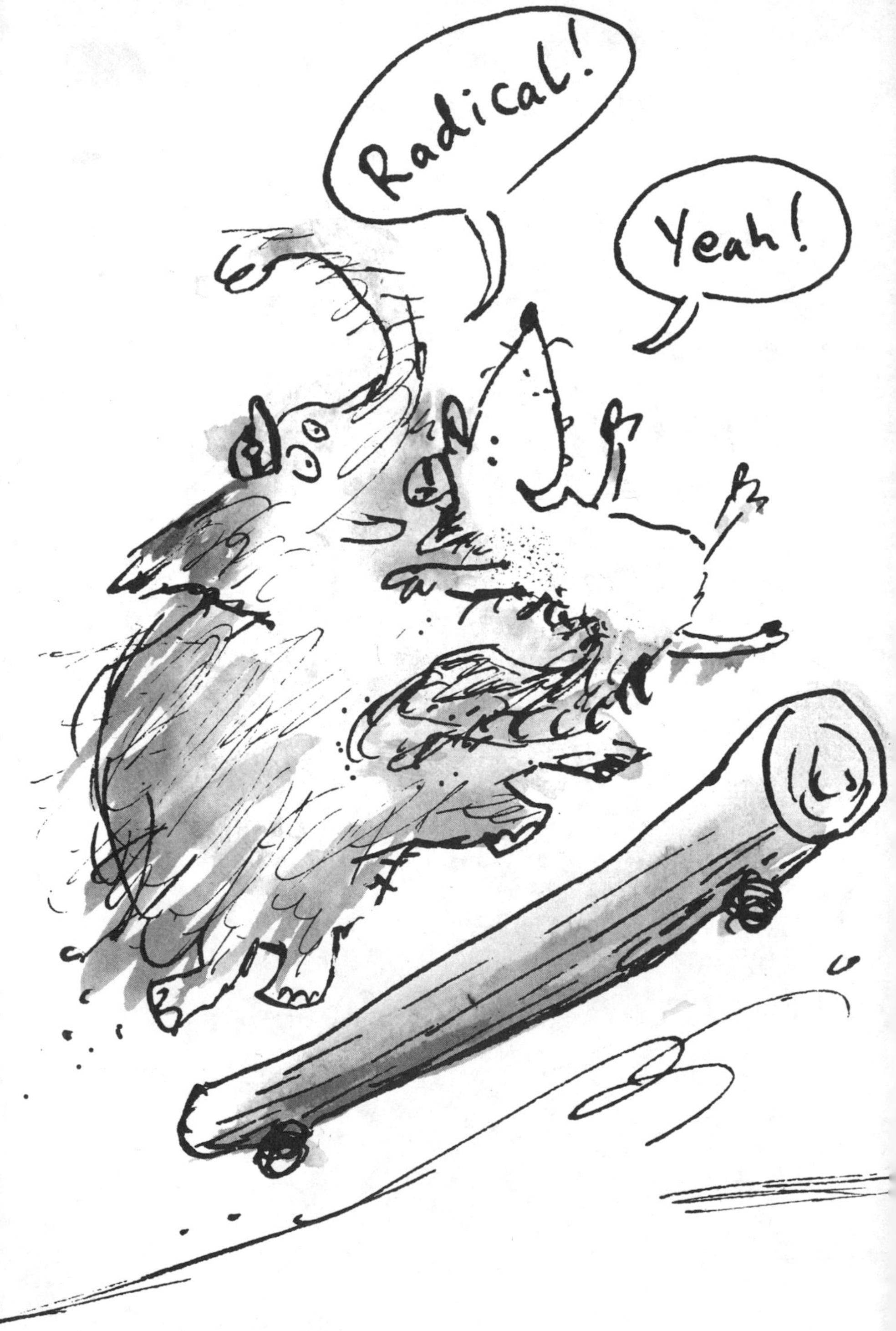
Radical!
Yeah!

10.
CRASHHH!

This was quite possibly the best thing Oscar or Fox had ever done in their lives.

The invention was now traveling at breakneck speed down the mountainside, spraying slush and mud all over its riders. Every now and then they would hit a bump and go flying high above the treetops before coming crashing down again. They were totally covered in leaves and grass, sopping wet with snow and mud, and gaining momentum all the time.

To turn, Oscar or Fox had to shout "LEFT!" or "RIGHT!" and then they would both lean over as far as they could.

CRASH!

Meanwhile, the human hunting party continued its march down the mountainside toward the
Academy.

The first the humans knew of Oscar and Fox's
pursuit was the sound of trees and bushes being
uprooted higher up the mountain. Then the smell
of Fox hit them.

And suddenly it burst into view. The biggest, smelliest, scariest, noisiest, fastest, mud-covered, four-eyed monster they had ever seen.

The humans started to flee its approach.

Oscar and Fox were amazed at how fast humans could run if they needed to.

"You wouldn't have thought their little legs could go that quickly," observed Oscar. By now they had emerged from the forest and were herding the humans directly toward the cliff.

"Erm, what happens when we get to the cliff?" asked Fox. But Oscar didn't have time to answer.

The humans reached the edge of the cliff and plopped straight over the edge. They would rather jump off a forty-foot cliff into a frozen marsh than face the hideous, smelly, scary, giant, speeding monster bearing down on them.

Oscar and Fox hit the edge of the cliff considerably faster than any of the humans.

Woooooooooo!

As they were catapulted high into the air, the humans far below them flailed waist-deep in the icy mud, covering their eyes and moaning in fear.

Oscar and Fox had never flown this high and in these circumstances. They found it wonderful. They seemed to be flying over the entire marshy marsh, heading toward . . .

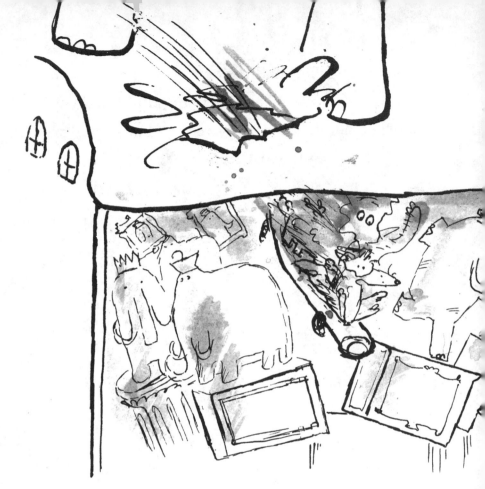

. . . the Academy!

CRASSHHHHHH!!!

They hit the ancient ice roof first and then smashed through two floors of empty storage space before finally landing in the Great Hall of Mammoth Sculptures. Professor Snout, who had been admiring a statue, was completely speechless.

But once he understood what was happening, he snapped into action.

BONG! BONG! BONG! The special alarm gong was sounded.

All those animals who weren't completely bed-ridden with sniffles were immediately called up to defend the Academy.

A party of mammoths was sent out to hurl as many snowballs as mammothly possible into the marsh to drive the humans back up into the forest.

The humans, already panicky and covered from head to toe in snow and marshy marsh mud, did not need much encouragement. They turned tail and fled as fast as they could.

That evening a special meeting was called.

Oscar and Fox were commended for saving the Academy. And everyone else was praised for snapping to attention and being really good at making tons of snowballs.

A special feast was prepared to celebrate their victory. Cook baked a special cake for the occasion. She even managed to find some oranges and cherries to serve with it, to make sure that everybody got a daily ration of fruit and nobody got the sniffles again.

Oscar and Fox were the guests of honor at the feast. Fox surprised everyone by taking a shower beforehand. In fact, Arabella and Prunella hardly recognized him when they presented the brave friends with bunches of flowers.

The rabbits performed some special music while Cave Bear and Owl sang a special song, and Ormsby and Giant Sloth performed a special dance.

Everyone joined in the party and ate—LOTS!

It was mammoth-tastic!

11.
FINALLY!

Lessons were cancelled for the rest of the year. Instead, the pupils spent their time rebuilding the Academy. With so many helping paws and trunks, it didn't take long. There was no more trouble from the humans, who were probably still recovering from shock.

And forever after, one day each year, all the animals were allowed to get as SMELLY as possible in honor of the brave rescuers. Nobody ever outdid Fox though: He really was the stinkiest.